Attention, Reader!

This book can be read frontward or backward!

But, whichever way you begin, you'll need to read <u>both</u> front and back <u>before</u> you read the final section in the middle. Otherwise, you won't be able to solve the mystery!

Oh, and by the way, as you read this book, please watch for signs like this one: . This will be a signal that I need to speak to you.

And you alone.

I promise we shall meet again soon!

—Ghostwriter

D0048403

THE LEGEND OF HAUNTED HILL

"I ran into Mom while I was exploring this afternoon," said Rob. "I got her to tell me the whole story. It seems this guy Hunt lost all his money in the great stock market crash of 1929. All he had left was this mountain and his dog, Buck. Hunt was a real weirdo. Didn't like trespassers. Most people stayed away . . ."

"Look," Max began. "This probably isn't such a good idea. You're going to get yourselves all—"

"We'll be fine," Lenni insisted. "We don't scare that easy."

"C'mon," Jamal said. "Tell us."

Rob lowered his voice. We all moved closer to the fire.

"It started last year," he said.

"What started?" Lenni asked.

"The haunting . . ."

STEER CLEAR OF HAUNTED HILL
A Bantam Book / July 1993

Ghostwriter, **Ghost**writer *and ● are*
trademarks of Children's Television Workshop.
All rights reserved. Used under authorization.

Art direction by Marva Martin
Cover design by Susan Herr
Interior Illustrations by Eric Velasquez

All rights reserved.
Copyright © 1993 Children's Television Workshop.
No part of this book may be reproduced or transmitted
in any form or by any means, electronic or mechanical,
including photocopying, recording,
or by any information storage and retrieval system,
without permission in writing from the publisher.
For information address: Bantam Books.

If you purchased this book without a cover you should be
aware that this book is stolen property. It was reported
as "unsold and destroyed" to the publisher and neither
the author nor the publisher has received any payment
for this "stripped book."

ISBN 0-553-48087-1

Published simultaneously in the United States and Canada

Bantam Books are published by Bantam Books, a division of
Bantam Doubleday Dell Publishing Group, Inc. Its trade-
mark, consisting of the words "Bantam Books" and the por-
trayal of a rooster, is Registered in U.S. Patent and
Trademark Office and in other countries. Marca Registrada.
Bantam Books, 1540 Broadway, New York, New York 10036.

PRINTED IN THE UNITED STATES OF AMERICA

OPM   0   9   8   7   6   5   4   3   2   1

Steer Clear of Haunted Hill

BY
ERIC WEINER

ILLUSTRATED BY
ERIC VELASQUEZ

A
CHILDREN'S TELEVISION WORKSHOP
BOOK

BANTAM BOOKS
NEW YORK · TORONTO · LONDON · SYDNEY · AUCKLAND

Attention, Reader! ☝

This book can be read frontward or backward!

But, whichever way you begin, you'll need to read <u>both</u> front and back <u>before</u> you read the final section in the middle. Otherwise you won't be able to solve the mystery!

Oh, and by the way, as you read this book, please watch for signs like this one: ☝. This will be a signal that I need to speak to you.

And you alone.

I promise we shall meet again soon!

—GHOSTWRITER

ALEX'S DIARY

El Diario Privado de Alejandro Fernandez
(Translation: The Private Diary of
Alex Fernandez)

(Extra translation: Anyone who reads this diary—
other than Ghostwriter, of course—will be subject
to a terrible curse! Alex's curse: May your whole
body be instantly covered with *ampollas y furunculos*
[a lot of blisters and boils]!)
(Extra extra translation: Gaby, this means you!
Keep out!!!!!!)

Thursday, 10:21 P.M.

Dear Diario,
   I don't know how I'm going to sleep tonight, I
really don't. Tomorrow the whole Ghostwriter
team is going camping at Hunt's Hill, in upstate
New York!
   The trip was Max Frazier's idea. Max is this cool

HUNT'S HILL CAMPGROUND

Monahatchee River

Lodge

Cabins

Waterfall

Baseball Field

Woods

Hunt's Hill

Tree house

Hunt's Cave

jazz drummer who lives above my father's *bodega* (that's Spanish for grocery store). Max is also my friend Lenni's dad. Anyway, years ago he went camping at Hunt's Hill Campground, and he loved it so much, he's always been meaning to go back there. He says there's a cave!

A cave—it will probably be so dark and spooky that only I will be daring enough to go in and explore.

And there's a mountain with an amazing view and—check this out—a waterfall!

The closest thing I have seen to a waterfall in Fort Greene, Brooklyn, is when the kids open up the fire hydrant and let it gush out into the street.

Max still has an old map of the place, which he gave to me. . . .

I gotta go. I share this room with my younger sister, Gaby. We *have* a shade down the middle of the room, but Gaby is complaining that my flashlight is making scary shadows. I mean, really.

That's the one bad thing I can think of about this trip. Since Max is taking the *whole* Ghostwriter team, Gaby is going too! Well, see you tomorrow. Alex

Friday, 12:21 P.M.

Dear Diario,

We're on the road! I've been looking forward to

this trip so long, I can hardly believe it's really starting. Max rented this big blue van. I'm in the front seat, which I claimed as soon as Max drove up. Surprise, surprise—sitting beside me is none other than my sister, Gaby, who insisted on being in the front and having the window seat, and when I complained she almost had a fit. I have to be careful she doesn't look over my shoulder while I write this, but if she thinks I'm going to spend all my time with her on this trip, she's got another think coming.

Lenni, Jamal, and Tina are sitting in the back. Jamal's grandmother, Grandma CeCe, and Rob are sitting in the very back. They have room for one more back there—why can't Gaby sit with them?

Great. Max just asked me to stop writing and keep my eyes peeled for the turnoff to Hunt's Hill Campground, so I gotta run!

I'm back. Guess what? Gaby says she's going to watch, so I can keep writing. I have to admit that was nice of her. It almost makes up for the extra equipment Gaby insisted we bring, and which *I* have to carry, like those stupid walkie-talkies for her and Tina. I'm sure those are going to come in real handy.

Not!

Anyway, I don't want to have a lot of equipment

with me. I plan to face the dark woods on my own, using only my wits and my bravery. Max says there are big bears that roam in this forest. Powerful bears that can kill you with one little swipe of their huge sharp-clawed paws.

Not that I'm afraid. Not for a second. Not Alejandro. I can see it now. We are all alone in the woods. At night. We hear a strange rustling. Gaby screams in terror. So does everyone else. Everyone except me.

Suddenly the ferocious animal charges.

"Don't be afraid, *mis amigos!*" I yell. Then I leap in front of the bear. It stops short, not sure whether to attack. I nail it with a steely glare. I am using the power of my mind to show it who is the boss. It works, of course. A moment later the bear turns and slinks away—

HUNT CAMPGROUND. TURN LEFT ON IVY LANE.

I'm back. Here's what happened. Max got annoyed with me for not watching for the turnoff to the campground. I said, "Gaby said *she* was watching." And Gaby said, "I was not! You were!"

Can you believe it?

Suddenly she let out a gasp. I looked down at my journal and saw the words and letters swirling around the page. "Look!" Gaby cried.

"What?" Max asked, glancing down. But, of course, he couldn't see it. Because only members of our team can see Ghostwriter's words.

I know, Diario, I haven't explained to you about this Ghostwriter friend of ours. The fact is, we don't really know who Ghostwriter is! We do know that he's this spirit who can read what we write and can write back to us. Right, Ghostwriter?

ABSOLUTELY CORRECT!

Lucky for us, Ghostwriter is on our side. He helps us when we get into trouble. And when you've got a younger sister, she can get you into trouble a lot!

Anyway, Ghostwriter rearranges letters he finds around him—on signs, in books, wherever he can get them—and writes to us. He wrote me the message you saw about Hunt's Hill Campground.

When I saw it, I said, "Oops. I think we missed the turnoff."

"You *think* we missed it?" said Max. But he turned the van around. I kept my eyes peeled for Ivy Lane. About ten minutes later I yelled, "I see it!"

Max slowed to a halt. "But which way do I go?" he wondered aloud.

"Left!" I called out.

"No, right!" said Gaby. (You know, I'm convinced that Gaby thinks she has to contradict me no matter what I say. If I said her name was Gaby, she'd say "Wrong!" and then she'd change her name to Maria so she'd be right!)

"Well, come on—which is it?" Max asked. "Left or right?"

Dear Diario,

My sister is only ten. I am thirteen. If I say we should go left, we should go left.

Of course, as it turns out, it was lucky we listened to her. I was correct that we were originally supposed to turn left, but that was when we were heading north. That's when Ghostwriter read the sign that said TURN LEFT. I forgot that since we were now coming back the other way, the directions were reversed.

Anyway, we turned right and soon came to a beat-up, rusted sign: HUNT'S HILL CAMPGROUND.

The whole ride up, Max had been worrying that the campground would be filled. He called ahead several times but got no answer. It wasn't worth the worry because now we were driving past one deserted cabin after another.

"Wow," said Jamal, "this place doesn't look too popular."

"Except as a place for some crazy escaped criminal to hide out in," agreed Lenni.

"Or wild beasts," Rob chimed in from the back.

"Stop it, you guys," warned Tina, covering her eyes. "You're scaring me."

I have to admit that I was a little scared. If you'll pardon the expression, Ghostwriter, the place looked like a ghost town!

"So? This way we'll have more privacy," Max said confidently. "It's a stroke of luck." But there was a worried look on his face.

Just then we barreled around a sharp turn in the dirt road and a large ramshackle building labeled LODGE loomed before us. Max parked. There were no other cars in sight. We all got out and stretched. The air was cool. It felt so clean you could almost taste it.

Gaby and Tina made us all pose for a group snapshot. I can tell you right now, Gaby, I'm not spending my whole trip posing for pictures.

Then Max started up the rickety wooden steps. The rest of us followed. Except for Gaby and Tina. They said they wanted to stretch their legs a bit more.

Right. They were just afraid to go in the lodge.

So was I, but I entered anyway. I half expected the lodge to be completely empty. Just a skeleton sitting behind the desk!

But instead we found a large woman with frizzy gray hair and a round, doughy face. She *was* sleeping, though.

"Ahem," Max said. But it was the screen door slamming shut behind Rob that woke her up.

She arose from her sleep, yelling.

"Oh, sorry," she said. "I was having a nightmare and . . . Well, I wasn't expecting any guests." Then she put on a big smile and added, "Welcome. I'm Mom. I run this campground."

The six of us all stood there, not looking too excited, I can tell you.

Then Jamal yelled, "All right!" He dropped his backpack and hurried across the lodge. "Look, guys, a video game!"

"See," Lenni told us, her brown eyes twinkling, "I knew Jamal would turn out to be a nature lover!"

"You know," Max was telling Mom, "no one answers your phone. I've been calling and calling and—"

Mom held up a hand. "Disconnected," she said sadly. "I'm afraid business has been kind of slow."

"Woman," said Grandma CeCe with a laugh, "from the looks of the cabins we saw coming in here, *dead* is more like it."

"But why?" Max asked. "This place used to be such a—"

"Used to be," agreed Mom ruefully. "But then people started worrying about the legend of Hunt's Hill. Or should I say, *Haunted* Hill."

"*Haunted*?" we all said together. Grandma CeCe turned and headed for the door. "Sorry, Mom," she said. "I don't even like nature. I'm sure not up for any ghosts. We're going to find another campground."

Grandma CeCe was joking, but Mom didn't laugh. "That's what everyone says," she said sadly.

"What's the legend?" Rob asked. You could tell from the way he asked that he wasn't scared. He was just planning on using it as background for one of those short stories of his.

"I probably shouldn't tell you," Mom said. She lowered her voice. We all stepped closer. Even Jamal had stopped inspecting the video game and was listening.

"It all started back in 1929," Mom began.

"In 1929!" we all repeated. Everything Mom said was beginning to strike us as scary.

"Right. That was the year of the stock market crash. A lot of millionaires lost all their money—and killed themselves. But this one man—"

The screen door slammed shut again. Grandma CeCe gasped. Lenni grabbed my arm.

Standing in the doorway was a tall, friendly-looking teenager with jet-black hair and a tight black T-shirt that read HUNT'S HILL CAMP-GROUND—STAFF. He looked about sixteen.

"You're not scaring these folks with that silly old legend, are you, Mom?"

"Well, Kyle, I—"

The teenager shook his head and laughed. "And you wonder why we have so little business." He smiled at us. "It's all nonsense," he said. "C'mon. You guys don't believe in ghosts, do you?"

Lenni and I exchanged glances. Not only did we believe in them, we had one for a best friend!

As you can imagine, we had our pick of the cabins. Max chose two that were close to the lake. I didn't like their names too much. The Windy Cottage and Cabin Fever. What are the other cabins in this joint? Death Hutch? Shack of Horrors? Anyway, I got one of the upper bunks in the boys' cabin, Windy Cottage. (That's where I'm writing from. And while I write, there's a spider spinning its web just a few feet above my head. Just my luck. Spiders freak me out.)

After we unpacked, Max said we could all have some free time to unwind before dinner. Rob went off to read one of the old paperbacks he had found in the lodge. I wanted to go rowing on the lake with Jamal. But I should have known what Jamal would want to do. Canoe the rapids? Hunt for buried treasure? No, he wanted to go back to the lodge

and try the video game. I didn't feel like rowing all by myself, so I went with him.

The game turned out to be Cave Explorer. You're this guy trying to find his way out of a dark, spooky cave filled with bats. I bet I'd be good at that in real life, but on a little video screen I bombed out. Jamal quickly mastered it, of course. When it comes to video games, that guy is the world's greatest athlete.

Anyway, Jamal was still on his fifth quarter, with no sign of losing, when he added his name as third highest scorer, under K. Garth and Mom.

Max just played the signal on this saxophone he brought on the trip just for fun. Time for dinner. *¡Adiós!*

Dear Diario,

I write to you by the light of our crackling campfire. Rob keeps poking it with this stick, trying to get the glowing coals to burn a little longer. We're the only ones left out here. I'm only going to write as long as Rob stays up, I can tell you that right now.

Listen to what happened. Jamal and I were gathering wood for the fire. Suddenly I saw Jamal stop short. He was looking straight down. He seemed to be frozen.

"What's wrong?" I asked him.

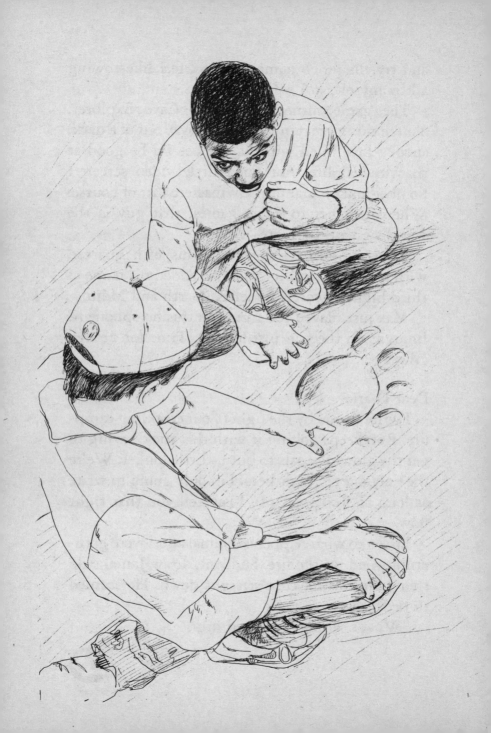

"Come here," he said, still looking down.

I went over to where he was standing. And dropped the armful of branches I was carrying.

At his feet was the biggest paw print I had ever seen.

"What is that?" I exclaimed.

"You're asking me?" Jamal said.

"Maybe it's from a dog."

"What kind of dog is that big?" Jamal asked.

"A very big dog," I joked.

"Look!"

Jamal pointed. There was another paw print a few feet ahead. We followed the tracks for several yards, then they disappeared into the brush. "Where was it headed?" I asked.

We both looked up in the direction of the tracks. Then we looked at each other. The tracks were leading straight toward Windy Cottage.

I'll tell you more about that creature in a minute.

First, though, I want to report that dinner was delicious. We roasted hot dogs and marshmallows. We brought them from New York, but they tasted so much better out here. Max says it's the air.

The mosquitoes are big and vicious here and they seem to like Grandma CeCe a lot. Even though she's been hogging the Bug Off. She keeps slathering the stuff on, slapping herself, and scratching. "I hate nature," she keeps muttering. "I hate it!"

Max led a sing-along with his saxophone. And then we started telling spooky ghost stories.

A lot of people are scared of the city, I know. But I live there, and as long as I can hear car horns and police sirens, I sleep like a baby. Up here, there is the eeriest silence.

Except for crickets. And other strange chirpings. And the sound of twigs breaking. Needless to say, we were all scaring ourselves pretty thoroughly.

Then Rob took his turn.

Like I told you, Rob is a great storyteller. "I don't know why we're bothering to *make up* stories," he said. "There's a real ghost story right here."

"Now, Rob," Max started, "you heard what that boy Kyle said. That's all just a legend—"

But Rob continued. "I ran into Mom while I was exploring this afternoon. I got her to tell me the whole story. It seems this guy Hunt lost all his money in the great stock market crash of 1929. All he had left was this mountain and his dog, Buck. Hunt was a real weirdo. Didn't like trespassers. Most people stayed away.

"Then one day some hunters were poaching on his property and they accidentally shot Buck."

Gaby screamed. We all nearly jumped out of our skins.

"What's the matter?" Grandma CeCe asked her.

"Sorry," she said. "I just got nervous, that's all."

"Look," Max began again. "This probably isn't such a good idea. You're going to get yourselves all—"

"We'll be fine," Lenni insisted. "We don't scare that easy."

Just then, Grandma CeCe slapped herself. Everyone jumped again.

"C'mon," Jamal said. "Tell us."

Rob lowered his voice. We all moved closer to the fire.

"It started last year," he said.

"What started?" Lenni asked.

"The haunting."

"I'm going home," Gaby announced. But she didn't move. None of us did.

"Last year," Rob went on, "people started reporting a strange sound on Hunt's Hill. The sound of a wild dog howling."

I found myself staring straight across the campfire at Jamal. Our eyes locked as the flickering fire lit up our frightened faces. "Did you say a wild dog?" Jamal asked.

Rob nodded. "That's not all. Hikers say they've seen Hunt's ghost."

There was silence as that news sank in.

"And the ghost of his dog," Rob added.

The silence deepened.

"You're all being very silly," Max said with a chuckle. "Now you all must be pretty tired, so let's—"

"Alex and I have seen the tracks of the dog's ghost," Jamal announced.

"What?" said everybody at once.

We explained what we'd seen.

"Guys," Max said, "that wasn't a ghost. This is the woods, remember? There *are* big wild animals around here."

"Oh, that makes me feel so much better," Lenni grumbled.

"Then came the accidents," Rob said.

"Puh-lease," Tina said, covering up her ears, "no more."

"Two canoers went over the falls and were badly hurt," whispered Rob. "Another group of campers went into the woods and got lost for days. When they were finally found, they said someone—or some*thing*—had been following them. They said it was like the ghost was luring them into danger."

Now Gaby also had her hands over her ears.

"I thought you kids were smarter than this," Max said. "Accidents will happen. That doesn't mean that this place is haunted." He gave us all a big smile. "Listen. Tomorrow morning I'm going to get up early and hike up Hunt's Hill. The view there is breathtaking, let me tell you. Now, who wants to join me?"

Just then, we heard the eerie sound of a dog howling in the distance.

No one volunteered for Max's hike.

Saturday, 10:15 A.M.

Dear Diario,

Major trouble. It's Saturday morning, and we're having a team rally. A rally is a kind of emergency meeting of the Ghostwriter team. I was picked to take the notes this time, so Ghostwriter can follow along with what's going on.

When we woke up this morning, Max was gone. We found this note.

Hey, you guys,

It's six o'clock. I can't believe you're all still in bed!

I'm off to climb Hunt's Hill. I'll yodel from the top and wake you all up.

Love,
Your Fearless Leader (Max)

The thing is, if he left at six o'clock, he should

have been back here long ago. But there's no sign of him. And no one has heard any yodeling, that's for sure.

Rob said he looked for Mom in the lodge but couldn't find her. Gaby said she was talking to Kyle earlier, but now she doesn't know where he is. So there's no one around for us to report that Max is missing.

Lenni wants to call a park ranger or something. But Gaby reminded us that the phone was disconnected.

Now what?

Where is Max?

Dear Diario,

We're out looking for Max in the woods. Lenni, Jamal, and I are taking a break while we wait for the rest of the group to catch up with us. So I thought I'd give you an update.

We waited for half an hour. Everyone was sure that at any second Max would come out of the woods, giving us that big grin of his. Or we thought we'd hear him yodeling from the top of Hunt's Hill.

But with every passing minute we began to get more and more worried. And there still was no sign of Max. So we all set off on our search. Just outside of camp Jamal found a trail of Max's sour-cream-

and-onion potato chips. It led to a path in the woods. We've been following that path for about an hour now.

What could have happened to him?

I don't want to say this out loud and scare Lenni, but maybe he slipped and fell or something. Maybe his leg is trapped under a giant rock. Maybe a big poisonous snake is slithering toward him. Suddenly, Alejandro bursts through the woods and grabs the snake and . . .

Uh-oh. Lenni is yelling at me.

She's worried that the second half of our group is now missing, too!

"Gaby!" I yelled.

"Tina!" Jamal hollered.

"Grandma CeCe! Rob!" shouted Lenni.

Then we waited. And listened to the silence.

"I don't believe it," Lenni said. "What's going on here?"

"They just fell behind," I assured her. "They'll be here any second." But what I was thinking about was what Rob had told us. About the legend. About the mysteriously disappearing campers.

We hollered some more. No response again.

Jamal wiped the sweat from his forehead with the back of his hand. "I don't like it," he said.

"I'm crazy about it," Lenni said.

"Seriously," Jamal said. "I think we lost them."

We hollered again. My throat was getting hoarse.

"Where could they have gone?" Lenni asked.

"It's like the woods swallowed them up," said Jamal.

"Jamal," I warned. "Don't try to scare us."

"I mean it," he said. "Look, first it was Max. Now half of our group is gone. These woods are haunted, man."

At the mention of her missing father, Lenni's eyes got all teary. I put my hand on her shoulder. "Lenni," I said, "don't start getting all worked up. You know your dad. He's probably daydreaming or reading a book or writing some music up on top of the hill. He probably just lost track of time and—"

I didn't finish. Because Jamal was yelling, "Look!"

I looked at where he was pointing. Way off in the thick of the woods was a cabin.

I flipped back through my journal to Max's map. There was no mention of the cabin. "Maybe Max saw this place and stopped there," I said.

"C'mon!" Lenni said. She headed off the trail into the thick of the forest. She had to bend back a thin tree branch to make her way through.

Thwap! It smacked me right in the chest.

"Sorry," she called. But she kept going, and Jamal and I followed.

Then she stopped. "It's gone," she said in amazement.

We stared into the dark of the forest. The cabin had disappeared!

"Maybe it was a mirage," Jamal said.

"It was no mirage," Lenni said. "We all saw it."

"Lenni's right. It's just out of sight," I said. "C'mon."

We headed on in what we hoped was still the right direction. Suddenly we came into a clearing. And there was the cabin.

Like every other building at Hunt's Hill Campground, the cabin looked totally deserted. The windows were dark, dead. The paint had long since peeled off the wood.

But there was smoke coming out of the chimney.

"Thank goodness," Lenni said. "At least there's someone here who can help us."

Jamal went first. We followed him. He stopped about halfway to the cabin.

"Hello? Anybody home?" he called. He must have had the same strange sense that I had. This was no ordinary cabin.

"I'm getting the creepiest feeling," Jamal said.

"Me too," I admitted.

"Like maybe we don't want to find out who lives here."

"Like maybe a ghost lives here," I agreed.

"Get real, you guys," Lenni said. She strode on ahead and rapped on the door.

There was no answer. We pushed on the wooden door. It swung open and banged against the wall. We peered into a dark room.

"Hello?" Jamal said again.

"We're lost," Lenni announced, as if someone were listening. "Can you help us?"

"I'm telling you," I said, "no one lives here."

"Then what about the smoke?" Lenni asked.

"The ghost," whispered Jamal.

"*¡Buenos días!*" I called. "*¡Estamos perdidos!*" My friends gave me an odd look. "Maybe it's a Spanish ghost," I explained.

"Check this out!" Lenni exclaimed. She had stepped into the cabin and was studying something on the wall.

We followed her in. What she was looking at were clippings of newspaper articles. Old ones, yellowed with age, from the 1920's.

" 'Millionaire Ed A. Hunt relaxes in his mountain cabin with his faithful companion, a golden retriever named Buck,' " Lenni read aloud. The photograph showed a tall, gaunt man with a dark mustache and burning eyes, who was petting his large dog.

"This must have been Hunt's cabin," I said.

I kind of wanted to get out of there, if you want to know the truth. The place gave me the *escalofríos* (the shivers)! But Lenni wanted to know where the smoke was coming from, so she went into the next room.

And let out a yell.

Dear Diario,

In the next room was a fireplace with some logs burning in it. A rocking chair was rocking slowly. But that could just have been because Lenni had brushed past it on her way into the room.

What she was pointing at was a message written in red on the wall. It looked like dried blood. And what the words said wasn't too comforting either.

Stay Out of My Woods! Ed A. Hunt

We ran out of the cabin and headed back toward the path. Except I think we must have gone the wrong way, because now we're totally lost. We've been resting by this little stream and—

ANAGRAM.

Is that you, Ghostwriter? What do you mean,

anagram? When you rearrange the letters to make a new word? An anagram of what?

AN ANAGRAM OF ED A. HUNT. PERHAPS IT'S NOT IMPORTANT. MAYBE YOU'VE JUST GOTTEN ME FRIGHTENED WITH ALL THESE MESSAGES ABOUT EVIL GHOSTS, BUT . . .

What? We can't guess the anagram. Tuna Hed? Date Hun?

Attention, Reader! 🏁
Before you read on, can you figure out an anagram of the name Ed A. Hunt?
—Ghostwriter

Dear Diario,

I think we're more lost than before, if that's possible. This backpack I'm carrying is starting to feel like it weighs about a hundred tons. I'm so glad I brought all this stuff for Gaby! Anyway, we're taking another rest stop. On some rocks. In the middle of nowhere.

As worried as we are about Max, and Gaby and Grandma CeCe and Rob, and Tina, we're starting to have a new worry.

Us.

Maybe Max and the rest of the group are all together somewhere looking for *us*. And that anagram Ghostwriter came up with isn't helping our mood any, I can tell you.

Ed A. Hunt = Haunted.

That's all we needed. I hope Ghostwriter is right about his getting carried away with this evil-ghost-legend business. It's after one o'clock, and we have no idea how to find our way out of the woods. At least in Brooklyn there are street signs and people you can get directions from or—

Sorry about the interruption. Jamal just spotted this sign behind where we're sitting. Lenni's taking a Polaroid of it.

PRIVATE WOODS! TRESPASSERS WILL BE SHOT! ED A. HUNT

Dear Diario,

"Well, let's just start walking," Jamal suggested.

"Which way?" Lenni asked.

"What's the difference?" I said. I started walking in any old direction.

I picked the wrong direction, though.

Because just then I heard a kind of whistling sound. This arrow zipped past my ear and *thwonk*ed into the tree trunk right next to me. The arrow's red feathers quivered in front of my nose.

Now it was my turn to yell. Then we all turned and ran.

The trees were pretty thick. It was hard to run fast. Still, we ran *very* fast.

Right into—

A man with a gun.

"Whoa!" he said. "Not so fast!"

We were all breathing hard. It took a moment to realize that the large man standing before us was wearing a light green uniform. The badge pinned to his shirt pocket read PARK RANGER— STEVE MORROW.

"Where are you kids running to?" he asked us. He stroked his dark mustache. Underneath the mustache was a friendly grin. My racing heart began to slow down.

"The arrow!" I gasped.

"The ghost is after us!" cried Jamal.

"Haunted!" Lenni threw in.

The ranger laughed and held up a hand. "You still need to slow way down," he told us.

We all tried to catch our breaths. I pointed back in the direction we had just come. "There must have been poachers," I said. "They shot at us with arrows."

The ranger's smile disappeared instantly. "Thanks," he said. "That's exactly who I'm out here hunting for." He put his hand firmly on my shoulder. "You see that little pile of three stones?"

I looked at where he was pointing. There they

were, three little rocks piled in a pyramid. I nodded.

"It's called a cairn," the ranger explained. "That's a trail marker. If you follow that trail, it will lead you straight back to the lodge."

"My father is missing," Lenni blurted out.

"And the other half of our group, too," Jamal added.

"Okay," the ranger said. "Don't worry. I'm going to go after those poachers, but I'll have my partner radio for help."

Don't worry. That's what he said. And for a while it helped. But that was two hours ago. We followed the trail of stone markers only to lose it again almost immediately.

Now we're facing a wide river. And a waterfall.

And even if we made it across the river, there's Hunt's Hill, rising high above us.

According to my map, we have now gone completely out of our way.

We could go back. But as Jamal says, for all we know, those poachers could be right behind us. With more arrows.

Aren't poachers supposed to shoot at animals, not at kids? Not these poachers. I have a feeling that if they catch us, it's *hasta luego*—see ya later for all of us.

Oh, no. I've gotta run.
Lenni is missing!

MORSE CODE

ALPHABET

A	.-	N	-.
B	-...	O	---
C	-.-.	P	.--.
D	-..	Q	--.-
E	.	R	.-.
F	..-.	S	...
G	--.	T	-
H	....	U	..-
I	..	V	...-
J	.---	W	.--
K	-.-	X	-..-
L	.-..	Y	-.--
M	--	Z	--..

NUMERALS

1	.----	6	-....
2	..---	7	--...
3	...--	8	---..
4	....-	9	----.
5	.....	0	-----

S O S S O SB U C R I S
... --- ... ... --- ... -... ..- -.-. .-. .. ...

A F TER M E
.- ..-. - . .-. -- .

31

Dear Diario,

No, I didn't suddenly forget how to write. That's code. But before I tell you about it, I have to tell you what happened next.

We found Lenni right away. Or she found us. She started shouting to us a second later.

Jamal and I rushed along the riverbank. We found her wading out into the river, then tugging on something large and silvery.

"What is it?" Jamal yelled. "What did you find?"

Lenni didn't answer. We kept hurrying toward her. "Help me!" she called, when we got closer.

We both splashed into the water. The falls were roaring in our ears and making the water all white and frothy. Now I could see what Lenni was pulling on. An aluminum canoe. What was left of it, anyway. The front third of the canoe was jammed in between two large mossy boulders. The rest of the canoe was dented and twisted.

We helped Lenni pull the canoe free and dragged it toward the shore.

"What do you want with this?" I asked her. "I hate to tell you, but we're not going to be able to paddle anywhere in this."

Lenni answered my question by silently pointing into the bottom of the damaged boat.

A small Polaroid camera and two waterlogged and broken walkie-talkies lay there.

We looked at one another without saying a word. Then Jamal finally said, "Are they . . . ?"

Lenni nodded. "That's Tina's camera."

"And Tina and Gaby's walkie-talkies," I added. Suddenly I felt as if a ton of bricks had just been loaded onto my stomach. I looked around wildly. "Gaby!" I screamed.

I didn't know what I was doing. But I waded back out into the water.

"Careful!" Jamal yelled.

A terrible current caught me around the legs and tried to drag me farther into the water. Jamal was jumping from rock to rock. He reached down and grabbed my hand. I made my way up onto the rock next to him.

Lenni was hopscotching her way from rock to rock as she moved farther away from the falls. "Tina! Gaby! Rob! Grandma CeCe!" she yelled.

It couldn't be. That's all I could think. It couldn't be.

Then Jamal shouted. He was pointing to a tree branch that hung down right into the river. Snagged on the branch was one of our group's Ghostwriter pens. We all carry them on cords

around our necks so we can write to Ghostwriter anytime we want.

When we were all back on shore, we stared at one another helplessly. I was horrified. I felt all hollow inside, like someone had just kicked me in the stomach.

"Okay, it's just like you guys have been telling me about my dad," Lenni told me. "They're okay. There's got to be some simple explanation for all this. I mean, this doesn't mean . . . " Seeing the expression on my face, she broke off.

"What do we do now?" Jamal asked.

"Maybe that ranger is still nearby," Lenni suggested.

A moment later we were all screaming for help. We screamed until our throats ached. And when we stopped, the only sound we heard was the sound of the falls crashing steadily down.

Jamal stared up at the sky. The sun was beating down on us. Then he gave a holler. "Smoke!"

He was right. There was smoke. And it was coming from the peak of Hunt's Hill.

We started shouting again.

"This is dumb," Lenni said. "Look how high that peak is. There's no way anyone up there could hear us."

"Anyway, the smoke stopped," I said, shading my eyes with my hand.

Jamal looked up. "It did not."

"It started again," I said with a shrug.

"And stopped again," said Jamal.

"And started again," I observed.

"Stop, start, stop?" Lenni said. It was like a light bulb went on over her head. "Are you thinking the same thing I'm thinking?" she asked us.

"I'm thinking you have an idea," Jamal said.

"What if it's code?" she continued, staring back up at the top of Hunt's Hill. "You know, Morse code."

"I thought that was for telegraphs," I said.

"It is, but you can do it with smoke, too," Lenni explained, "with anything that can be used to make short and long signals. See that quick puff of smoke? That could be a dot. And that long one? That could be a dash!"

"Quick!" Jamal told me. "Copy it down."

I grabbed my journal and jotted down the dots and dashes as Lenni and Jamal called them out. Then we all looked at what I had written.

"Lenni," I said. "You forgot one thing. None of us knows Morse code."

"None of us?" Jamal said, raising his eyebrows.

Lenni must have known what he was thinking, because she grabbed a stick and wrote in the sand, "GW—Morse code?"

A few moments later Ghostwriter's message appeared in my diary. Ghostwriter had written out the alphabet. And next to the alphabet were sets of dots and dashes.

"All right!" said Jamal. "So let's see. The message starts out dot dot dot, dot dot, dot dot dot. . . ."

"That's SOS!" Lenni cried, staring down at my diary.

Attention, Reader! ⊙
Turn back to my Morse code chart and the message that Alex copied down.
Can you translate it?
—Ghostwriter

Pretty soon we had all the letters translated. SOSSOSBUCKISAFTERME. When I broke the letters up into words, we had our message: SOS! SOS! Buck is after me!

"Buck?" Jamal said, his eyes wide.

An image flashed into my mind. It was that huge paw print Jamal had found when we were looking for wood last night. Then I pictured the dog in the newspaper photos at Hunt's cabin.

"Hunt's dog?" Lenni asked. "From the 1920's?"

The smoke signals had stopped. Somehow the clear blue sky looked scary to me now.

"C'mon," Jamal urged.

He jumped out onto one of the nearby rocks and started making his way across the river.

We didn't need to ask where he was going.

Getting across the river was hard enough. Getting up Hunt's Hill proved to be a nightmare.

It is now a couple of hours later. We are still only about halfway up the hill. It's really more of a mountain, if you ask me! I am covered with scratches and bug bites and sweat and dirt. I guess there must be trails for going up this thing, but we sure haven't found any.

The only thing that's keeping me going is the thought that maybe it was Gaby who had made those smoke signals.

But if it was her—if she had survived that canoe crash—then she was the one signaling SOS. And that means my *best* hope is that she's the one in trouble!

Jamal has been leading the way. A few minutes ago, he just stopped, slipped off his backpack, and lay down, exhausted. Lenni and I did the same.

But I don't think we're going to rest much longer. From the looks of it, I think the sun is beginning to set.

"What do we do when it gets dark?" Lenni asked, staring up at the sky.

"Use our flashlights," Jamal answered simply.

The thought of being lost and alone in the

woods in the darkness seemed to revive us all pretty fast.

"*Vámonos,*" I said, getting back to my feet. Jamal and Lenni didn't move. "That means let's go," I translated.

"I know what it means," Lenni said without moving. "It's my body that doesn't understand."

I reached out a hand and she grabbed it and let me pull her up.

"*Vámonos,*" Jamal repeated, then got to his feet and started climbing again.

I was trying to force any dark thoughts out of my mind. Just put one foot in front of the other, I told myself.

But I kept thinking about Gaby and the shattered canoe. I couldn't help thinking that somehow I was being punished for being mean to her.

I apologize, Gaby! What I wouldn't give to have you bothering me right now!

We kept climbing. In a few minutes we came out of the woods. We weren't at the summit, but we were facing a wall of rock. And in that wall was a large, dark hole that seemed to beckon to us.

"The cave!" I cried. I flipped to my map and pointed to it. "Hunt's Cave."

We all stared at the jagged hole. It was like a black eye. It looked evil.

"I don't think we should go in there," Jamal said.

"Okay," Lenni said. "You wait out here while me and Alex explore it."

"No way," Jamal said. "You guys aren't going in, either!"

"Why not?" I asked. "Maybe Max is in there. Or Gaby."

"No, you're not going in," Jamal said, "because if you go in, *I* have to go in."

Lenni and I both managed a chuckle. Then Lenni started trudging toward the hole in the rock. "*Vámonos,*" she called back.

The entrance to the cave was very high, like a huge slash in the side of the hill. But it was narrow. We had to turn sideways to inch our way in.

"I can't believe I'm doing this," I heard Lenni say up ahead.

After about ten yards we came to a tunnel that was only about three feet high. We had our flashlights on, but it was still incredibly dark. It was the kind of darkness you can't get by closing the door of a room. This felt like darkness itself.

The tunnel opened into a huge cavern. We shone our flashlights upward and there seemed to be no end to it.

Then something moved through the darkness over our heads.

"I'm not going to scream," Jamal said calmly. "Just tell me that I didn't see what I think I saw."

"I'm afraid you did see what you thought you saw," Lenni said.

Jamal screamed. "Sorry," he said. "Bats are one of the few things that get to me. It won't happen again." Then he screamed again.

"How come you played that video game so well?" I whispered. "That was all about bats."

"Yeah, but I was pretty sure the bats weren't going to swoop off the screen and bite me," Jamal answered.

"Gaby told me that she read somewhere that bats are pretty harmless," Lenni said. "They would never fly into you on purpose or anything."

There was a flurry of wings as something flew right past our heads. We all screamed this time.

"It's almost night," Lenni explained. "These guys are just waking up."

"*Buenos días,*" I said. Then I yelled, "Gaby!"

Pretty soon we were all yelling out the names we had yelled so many times today. We got our usual answer. Silence. Except this time we heard the flutter of hundreds of leathery wings.

Jamal moved forward.

"Where are you going?" Lenni demanded.

"When your dad told me about this cave," Jamal said, "I think he said there's another chamber."

"Gee," said Lenni. "I wonder if it's as nice as this one!"

We picked our way over the rubble-strewn floor of the cave until we came to another narrow opening.

I went first. I had to bend over double. I was waving my hand around in front of me. Still my face went right into a spider's web.

"Gross!" When I got out of the tunnel, I flailed my arms and made spitting sounds.

"Easy!" Jamal said. I guess I was slapping him. I stopped.

"Sorry," I said.

Which was when I felt the spider crawling down my back.

I yanked my shirt up. "Get it off me!" I yelled. "C'mon! Get it off!"

Jamal found the spider with his flashlight and nudged it off. I was shaking. "What happened to all that stuff about not being scared?" Jamal asked me.

"That was bats," I explained. "Not spiders."

We were now in another huge chamber. We called again, but there was still no answer.

"Okay," Jamal said sadly. "Looks like another dead end. We can go now."

"I hate to leave," Lenni said. "I have such fond memories of this place."

Even after we came out of the cave, we had to keep our flashlights on. The sun had set while we were inside. It was as if being in the cave had darkened the whole world.

We found a narrow path that went around the rock face of the cave and into the forest. But soon Jamal said, "Let's rest," and we all groaned and fell to the ground in agreement.

So, where am I writing from right now?

I have no idea! Somewhere on Hunt's Hill.

It's pitch-black out. Mosquitoes are dive-bombing at us on all sides.

But that's the least of our problems. Because a few minutes ago we heard something howling. The howling of a wild dog . . . an angry dog . . . a ghost dog.

It was the same sound we had heard at the campfire last night. Only this time it's much, much closer.

Reader—Stop!

Alex's diary stops here!

Do not turn this page!

First turn the book over and read Gaby's diary. Then continue reading straight through to the end of the book. Otherwise you will not be able to solve the mystery.

Or if you have already read Gaby's diary, turn the book over, flip to page 43, and begin reading from there.

—Ghostwriter

GABY'S DIARY

▽

¡CUIDADO! CAUTION!

This diary is the totally private property of Gabriela Fernandez of Fort Greene, Brooklyn.

By the way, anyone who so much as peeks into this diary will expose himself or herself to el peligro de la muerte. *For those of you who don't speak Spanish, that's the danger of death!*

(Ghostwriter, this doesn't mean you!)
(Alex, this *does* mean *you!*)

Friday, 6:31 A.M.

Dear Pen Pal,
¡Buenos días! Good morning!

2

You know, all my life I've wanted a pen pal. Okay, I'm only ten years old, but still, I've wanted one all my life.

My older brother, Alex, has all these pen pals all over the world. He writes to them and they write back. So you, Diary, you will be my pen pal, my *amiga*. (That means girlfriend in Spanish. Can you speak Spanish, Pen Pal? Alex and I can because our parents were born in El Salvador.)

Anyway, I got up really early this morning. I didn't mean to, but suddenly my eyes just popped open and I thought, Wow! Today's the day!

Today's the day that Max Frazier, the jazz musician who is our upstairs neighbor, is taking the whole Ghostwriter team on a camping trip to Hunt's Hill Campground in upstate New York.

I know, Pen Pal, you are wondering, Who is this Ghostwriter person?! What do I mean by the Ghostwriter team? I have so much to tell you. Ghostwriter is—

I'm back. And I'm in trouble. See, I share a room with my older brother, Alex. Alex got mad because he says I woke him up and it's only six in the morning.

It serves him right, if you want to know the truth. Because last night he kept the overhead light on for thirty minutes *after* I begged him to

3

turn it off so he could write in *his* diary. And then he starting using his flashlight and it made these very creepy shadows on the shade that divides our room.

Also, Alex has to be the lightest sleeper ever born. I am hardly making noise at all.

Okay, okay. He's really getting mad now. I gotta go. I'll write again soon! *Hasta luego.* (See ya later!)

Your friend, Gaby

12:25 P.M.

What perfect weather for our trip! The sky is so blue it looks like the ocean. And we are riding in the belly of a great blue whale.

That's what I call it, anyway. Max rented this big blue van for the trip. I have named it the whale.

I'm sitting in the front seat next to Alex. Would you believe it? Alex made a big fuss about letting me sit here. As usual, he seems to have forgotten that he promised me I could have a window seat. I claimed it two weeks ago, as soon as I heard about the trip.

He was also griping that I brought too much stuff. Never mind the fact that he brought along four mystery novels! I can't believe he doesn't get tired of all those whodunits. He's read so many that once he read a Hardy Boys almost to the end before he realized that he had read it before.

The only book I brought along was a wilderness guide. Now *that's* something useful. As soon we were on the highway, I tested everyone from it. "Okay, guys," I yelled. "Pop quiz."

Alex groaned. "C'mon, Gaby, we're out of school now. That's the whole point of this trip. To get away."

But Jamal, who was in the main seat, said, "Hit it, Gaby. I know everything."

"All righty," I said. And I stumped him with my first question. "How many leaves does poison ivy have?"

My friend Tina Nguyen was sitting next to Jamal. Her hand shot up. "I know!"

"How many leaves?" said Jamal's grandmother, CeCe. "Too many leaves!"

Grandma CeCe was sitting all the way in the back with our team's newest member, this guy in Jamal and Alex's class, Rob Baker. He had his nose buried in a book—as usual. Alex says Rob is going to be a great writer someday, so it makes sense he's always reading. "Rob," I called. "Can we have your attention, please?"

Rob looked up from his book, surprised. "Sorry, Ms. Fernandez," he called back with a smile. "I guess my mind wandered."

Tina was waving her hand and bouncing up and down in her seat. "Oh, all right," I said. "Tina?"

"Poison ivy has three leaves."

"Right. They come in clusters of three leaves. Sometimes they have white berries. Now the next question—"

"The next question," Alex interrupted, "is what do you do after you're attacked by a raccoon with rabies that sinks its fangs into your flesh and takes a big bite out of you?"

"Alex, gross," said Lenni Frazier, pushing her long brown hair behind one ear.

"Jamal," Max called. "Are those potato chips you brought along plain? If they are, pass 'em on up here, would you?"

"I'm serious," Alex went on. "I was reading this magazine article about rabid raccoons. It's becoming a real problem at campgrounds just like the one we're going to."

"Mr. Frazier?" Tina called out. "Is that true?"

Max was happily munching on Jamal's plain potato chips and tapping the steering wheel in rhythm with the jazz tape he had in the tape deck. "Well," he called back, "raccoons are nothing you have to worry about. But it is important to remember that even if they look cute, you don't want to pet them or feed them. They're wild."

I shivered. But Alex continued, "The trouble is, if you *don't* feed them, that makes them even hungrier. There was a case of this grandmother who lived in upstate New York—"

"Don't you be talking about grandmothers, Alex," Grandma CeCe yelled from the backseat.

"A raccoon climbed down her chimney in the middle of the night while she was sound asleep—"

"Alex," I pleaded. "Please don't tell me about this."

Everyone yelled at Alex to stop it. Lenni made puking sounds. Jamal was clapping and laughing. What is it about boys? They think that anything gross is automatically funny.

I didn't want to give Alex the satisfaction of knowing he was scaring me. But he was.

I'LL PROTECT YOU, GABY.

Aw, Ghostwriter! That's so nice of you. I almost forgot you'd be coming on this trip. I feel better already.

Pen Pal, I promised to tell you about Ghostwriter. First of all, Ghostwriter is reading everything I write to you. But don't worry, you can trust him to keep our secrets.

We formed our team out of the kids that Ghost-writer has contacted. No one else can see his messages. We call him Ghostwriter because he rearranges our words and letters when he writes his messages to us, like that message he just sent me. We've never *seen* him, but we know this: He's on our side. I can't tell you how many times he's helped us out of tight spots.

Now Alex is writing in his diary, the copycat. My father gave us both identical diaries so we could record all of the interesting sights we see and the facts we learn. But I'll bet Alex is writing about me. He's got his shoulder all hunched up as if I would want to peek and see what he's writing. Believe me, Alex, I would never peek.

Unless, of course, I thought I could peek without you catching me!

Hmm . . . I'm getting a little carsick, so I better stop!

I'm back and feeling better.

It's amazing. Alex will blame me for anything. While I was writing my last entry, Max asked Alex to keep a lookout for the sign for the turnoff to the campground. I specifically told him that I *couldn't* watch the road because I was writing in

We Just got here!

my journal. Then, when we missed the turnoff, Alex said I had promised to watch.

As I keep telling him, he should just accept the fact that I am always right and then we'd have no more arguments.

Dear Pen Pal,

I've got a little time left before dinner. Sorry I haven't written in so long. What has it been? Over an hour!

When we drove into Hunt's Hill Campground, I was almost sorry I had a window seat, let me tell you. The place was totally empty. There were pad-locks on the cabin doors. No cars. No people. I kept imagining that I saw beady dark eyes staring back at me from every window. You know, rabid raccoons.

I'll bet these raccoons are bigger than I am! A horrible thought occurred to me. What if the rac-coons run this campground? What if they ate all the people long ago?

I felt better when we all piled out of the blue whale's belly in front of the lodge. There were still no cars or people in sight. But no raccoons, either. And it felt so good to be out of the car that all my worries vanished into the cool mountain air.

"Picture! Picture!" I yelled, clapping my hands.

"No way," Alex said. "We just got here."

"That's exactly why we need a picture," I said. "It'll be our 'just got here' picture."

Tina gave her Polaroid camera to Lenni and we all posed in front of the blue whale. "Say 'rabid raccoon,'" Lenni said. Which is why I made the awful face you see in the photo.

"Okay," I said. "Now one with Lenni."

"No way," Alex said, heading for the lodge. Sometimes I think he just doesn't like it when I make a suggestion. Any suggestion I make, his first response is no.

"Let's get registered and unpacked first," Max told me. He started for the lodge and the rest of the group followed.

"Tina, wait," I said. "How about another picture of me?"

Now that we were here I didn't feel like going *inside* for a long time. The green trees, the fresh air, the blue sky—they all made me feel like doing cartwheels.

Which is exactly what I did.

While I was in the air, I heard Tina yell.

And when I landed, I was looking straight up into the eyes of this incredibly handsome teenager. With jet-black hair. And these soft eyes—like a deer's.

"Sorry," Tina called. "I didn't mean to yell, but you came around the corner so suddenly."

11

The guy was laughing. "You scared *me,*" he said. He held out a hand. "My name's Kyle. I work here."

"Gaby Fernandez," I said, sticking my hand out. He shook it. Remind me never to wash my hand again.

Tina came running over. She did a cartwheel herself, wiped her hands on her jeans, then shook his hand as well. "Tina Nguyen." I could tell Tina felt the same way I did.

"How long are you staying?" he asked us.

"That depends," I said. "Is it true about the rabid raccoons?"

He arched an eyebrow. "Rabid raccoons?"

"We heard they were everywhere," Tina said.

Kyle laughed again. Every time he laughed, I felt better. "I've got signs up," he said, "warning you not to feed them. But aside from that, I'm sure you'll be fine." He headed for the lodge. "See ya around."

A few minutes later everyone came back out of the lodge. We got back into the blue whale and drove down toward the lake. It came into view suddenly as we rounded the corner, this splash of green and blue.

Max had rented two cabins, one for the boys and one for the girls. After we unpacked our stuff, he announced some free time before dinner. Tina and I immediately headed back to the lodge to see if we could run into Kyle.

We found him working behind the desk. "What can I do for you?" he asked, smiling down at us.

"Uh . . ." I said. We had forgotten to come up with a reason to look for him.

"Do you have any souvenirs?" asked Tina, saving the day.

"Souvenirs? Well, let's see. We have some postcards." He pointed to a small revolving rack on the desk beside him.

"Oooh, great," I gushed. Tina and I studied the postcards for a few minutes. I bought this one:

Hunt's Cave
Hunt's Hill, New York

WISH YOU WERE HERE!

Kyle

The vast three-chambered cave of Hunt's Hill draws crowds of spelunkers every year.

Alex was mad because I made him carry my dictionary in his backpack. It's a lucky thing I did, because I had to look up the word *spelunker*. It means cave explorer.

But it doesn't look like Hunt's Cave is drawing any crowds of spelunkers this year. I don't know why. Max told us that this was a really popular spot when he came here. Of course, that was about ten years ago. I also got this free map of the place, which they had a pile of on Kyle's desk.

You would think that with a waterfall and everything this place would be a lot more popular. Anyway . . .

Where was I? Oh, yeah. Tina and I were asking Kyle about the recreation equipment, which I could see on the loaded metal shelves behind him.

"You name it," he said, "we got it. You just have to sign it out." He gestured behind him. "We've got lifejackets, oars for the rowboats, and paddles for the canoes." He pointed out the bows and the quivers of red-feathered arrows. "We've got archery set up just behind the lodge. And Ping-Pong and badminton and—"

"Badminton!" Tina clapped her hands.

Kyle looked at me, and when I nodded, he gave us two rackets and a birdie. He took a piece of paper that was lying on the desk and quickly drew directions on the back. To get to the badminton

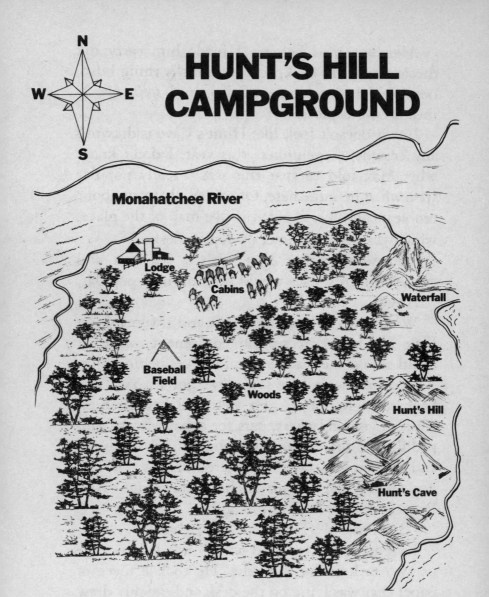

HUNT'S HILL CAMPGROUND

N
W E
S

Monahatchee River

Lodge

Cabins

Waterfall

Baseball Field

Woods

Hunt's Hill

Hunt's Cave

court, he told us, we had to go behind the lodge and around the maintenance shed and . . .

I wasn't listening anymore. I saw this little fuzzy ball hovering above the piece of paper. Kyle just kept talking, without batting an eye. That's because only members of our team can see Ghostwriter's signs, like I said.

The sign meant that Ghostwriter was reading something. But what? And why?

Dear Mom Brody,

I was sorry to hear that business has been so slow. And upset to hear you are thinking of selling. As you know, Hunt's Hill is close to my heart. I came here on my honeymoon in '73.

I'll do anything to make sure that this beautiful spot doesn't get ruined by developers like so many of the parks in this area. If you do decide to sell, I expect you to come to me first.

Let's talk.

Yours,
George Garth

Dear Pen Pal,

Okay, now I know what Ghostwriter was reading. He was reading the letter that was on the front of Kyle's directions. See, I copied it into my journal. When we get home, I'm going to paste Kyle's map in, too. Or I'll frame it and hang it on my wall.

Poor Mom. Tina and I met her on our way to the badminton net. She seems real nice—she's got these fat cheeks you just want to pinch—but she's also real sad.

I guess it makes sense that Mom has to sell this place, since business is so slow. But it still seems a shame.

Right now, I'm lying on one of the upper bunks of Cabin Fever. It's a good name for this place. Because I'm in a sweat.

It's time for bed, and we're taking turns going to the bathroom, which is several buildings away. Which means going through the pitch darkness. The last thing I want to do is go out there. Believe me, if I thought I could hold it all night, I would.

Grandma CeCe has the bunk underneath me. She keeps slapping mosquitoes and making jokes about how she never should have left Brooklyn.

Why am I in a sweat? I was having a great time until tonight's campfire. That's when Rob told us about the curse of Hunt's Hill.

Get this. The place is haunted. The Hunt in the name comes from a man named Hunt. He was this millionaire who lost all his money way back in 1929. He moved to a cabin in these woods, which were his last possession. He lived all alone with his dog, Buck. Then some poachers shot the dog.

Now the ghosts of Hunt and Buck are supposed to wander around the grounds preying on anyone who tries to camp out here!

Hunt's ghost is big. With this dark mustache and these haunted burning eyes. Rob said his eyes are enough to scare you to death. I'm so glad he added that extra detail. Rob says that details are what make a story come alive. That one sure worked.

Ghostwriter, do you believe in this legend? You don't, do you? Please tell me you don't.

I WILL READ WHAT I CAN ABOUT HUNT, GABRIELA. BUT, I MUST ADMIT, I *DO* BELIEVE IN GHOSTS!

Sorry, right, I forgot. Okay, Lenni just got back from the bathroom. That means it's Tina's turn. I'm going with her!

That does it. I'm going to be up all night. I know it.

We made it to the bathroom okay. Except inside there were all these bugs swarming around the light bulb. Moths. Huge mosquitoes. Tiny gnats. You name it.

Then, on our way back, I thought I heard something and I stopped short.

"What is it?" Tina whispered.

"Shhh!" We both listened. We heard leaves rustle behind us. We whirled around and beamed our flashlights into the woods. We couldn't see a thing. But just to be on the safe side, we started running.

We got as far as the campfire, which Rob and Alex had poured water on and put out completely. We stopped there because now it was Tina who heard something.

"Ay!" I cried.

"What?" said Tina. "Did something bite you?"

"No. You're digging your fingers into my arm!"

We started giggling. But then we heard something that shut us up pretty quick.

Snap.

It was a twig breaking.

We stood frozen, listening. "Did you hear that?" I asked.

"I hope not," said Tina.

Snap.

We knew what we were hearing. Animals. Wild animals.

"Look!" Tina was beaming her flashlight about twenty yards away. Caught in the beam was a pair of beady red eyes. A raccoon!

Another twig cracked behind me. I whirled and pointed my flashlight like a gun.

"Hey!" I said. There was another raccoon about ten yards behind us.

"They're circling us," Tina whispered.

It was true. The two raccoons were moving around slowly in a wide circle, their eyes never leaving ours.

"And they're getting closer!" I said.

I picked up a stick that Rob had used to poke the fire. "Let's make a run for it," I hissed to Tina.

Raising the stick over my head and giving a war cry, I started running for the cabin. Tina followed, yelling as well.

"Hey, keep it down out there!" Alex yelled from the other cabin.

Sure, I would have liked to hear the sound he would have made if they had been circling *him.*

We bounded up the rotten wooden steps to the cabin. And stopped short.

Because on the steps was another animal, staring right back at us.

The good news was, it wasn't a raccoon. The bad news was, it was a skunk. It had its tail up. It looked as startled as we were. The skunk climbed down the steps and headed off into the darkness. We ducked into the cabin, slammed the door behind us, and locked it.

"Boo!" Lenni sprang out at us. And we shrieked at the top of our lungs.

"Hey, guys, we're trying to sleep over here," Max called from the other cabin.

Lenni was on the floor laughing. But she stopped laughing when we told her what had happened.

"I hate this place," said Tina. "I mean, if Hunt's ghost doesn't get us, the wildlife will."

"Grandma CeCe, tell us the place isn't haunted," I begged.

Grandma CeCe was busy spraying the air with Bug Off. "It's haunted by mosquitoes," she said. "That's for sure." She chuckled ruefully. "The animals are just looking for a snack, same as these bugs."

I'm back in my bunk, writing this by flashlight. Every few seconds Grandma CeCe slaps herself really hard. Lenni says the light is bothering her, though, so I gotta go.

I'm going to be up all night. I know it.

Saturday, 10:02 A.M.

Dear Pen Pal,

¡Estoy muy cansada! That means I'm very tired. I don't know when I finally fell asleep last night. But when I did, I dreamed that I was still awake. Then I dreamed that the ghost of Hunt's dog was chasing me—right toward the edge of the waterfall.

Right now I'm lying on the bank of the river, doing a little sunbathing.

Okay, I also came down here to see Kyle. He's sunbathing not far away. I waved to him once, but I don't want him to think I'm looking at him.

Maybe I'll sneak one peek . . .

Hey! He's coming over here!

Cool! Kyle ate his breakfast with me. From what he ate I can tell that he is not exactly a health nut. He began with two frosted doughnuts, washed them down with a can of root beer, then moved on to (grossest of all) some beef jerky.

I was in the middle of telling him how the people of Latin America are all much healthier than the people of North America because they eat so much *arroz y frijoles*—rice and beans—when suddenly the letters on his bag of potato chips began to dance.

"What's the matter?" Kyle asked me.

I knew he couldn't see it. "Nothing," I said. "But I think I better go check what my team—" I was about to say teammates. "What my friends are up to," I said instead.

The letters on the potato chip bag were now flashing. LALLY'S SOUR CREAM AND ONION had become RALLY—L! plus the leftover letters SSOUCREAMANDONION.

"See ya!" Kyle said with a friendly grin. He settled back with his hands under his head. "If you guys need any equipment, you know where to find me."

"Thanks." As soon as I was out of sight, I started to run. Rally—L! Ghostwriter was telling me that Lenni was calling an emergency meeting.

I found everyone gathered in Windy Cottage. "What's up?" I asked when I saw their concerned faces.

Alex told me. Max had gone off hiking early this morning, just like he'd said he was going to do last night. Except that now he was very late in coming back and he might be in some kind of trouble.

"That's supposed to be part of the curse of Hunt's Hill," Rob said. "It makes people disappear, like the Bermuda Triangle or something."

"That's crazy and you know it," Jamal said quickly, looking at Lenni.

26

I knew what he was thinking. What if Max was gone forever?

Lenni has already lost one parent. Her mom died of cancer when she was seven. That's younger than I am now. I can't even begin to imagine what that would be like. I don't want to imagine it. I love Lenni. It must be so scary for her to even *think* her dad might be hurt.

Right after the meeting, I ran back down to the lake, but Kyle was gone. I checked the lodge too, but I couldn't find him.

Now we're just waiting a little longer to give Max a chance to come back. One minute I'm sure he's going to show up. The next minute I have the worst feeling. I don't even want to write it down. But somehow I feel like we won't be seeing Max for a long, long time.

Dear Pen Pal,

Tina just insisted we take another little rest stop. Which is a relief, I admit. This backpack is really heavy, even though I got Alex to take a lot of my stuff.

Still, I think we're falling too far behind Alex, Jamal, and Lenni.

At our first rest stop, Rob decided to go off on his own trail. He thought we'd have a better chance of finding Max if we spread out that way.

He's probably right. But I wouldn't want to be by myself in these woods, that's for sure.

I know my imagination is getting the best of me again, but I can feel something in these woods. Something not right. Something evil.

Dear Pen Pal,

As soon as we started hiking again, Grandma CeCe cried out. She had stepped in a hole and twisted an ankle.

Tina and I helped her to a tree stump. "Are you okay?" I asked. I knelt down and unlaced her sneaker.

"I'm fine," Grandma CeCe said, wincing. "I just can't walk. But walking is overrated, I always say."

Tina cupped her hands to her mouth and shouted, "Hey, guys, wait up! Grandma CeCe's hurt!"

There was no answer.

"Why don't you just shout out that CeCe's a klutz?" Grandma CeCe joked.

Tina and I shouted for help as loudly as we could. Grandma CeCe joined in. Still no answer.

"They must have gotten too far ahead," Tina said, frowning.

"Wait a minute!" I said. "Gaby to the rescue!" I zipped open the top of my backpack and yanked out my walkie-talkie. "Ta-da!"

"Fantastic," said Grandma CeCe, scratching her arms.

"Good thinking," agreed Tina.

"Alex made fun of me for bringing this," I told them. "Now I'll show him how useful it can be." I raised the antenna. The walkie-talkie crackled with static. "Alex! Come in, Alex!"

There was no answer. "I hope he's got his turned on," I said, worried.

Tina was giving me a kind of funny look. "Uh-oh," she said. She unzipped her backpack. And removed the other walkie-talkie.

"Hmm . . . bummer," I said.

"Do you think you can walk on it at all?" Tina asked Grandma CeCe.

"Let's see," she said. We helped her to her feet. She took one step, then plopped back down on the stump. Then she started scratching her arms again. "How many leaves did you say are on poison ivy?" she asked me. "Four, right?"

"Three!"

Grandma CeCe examined her arms closely. "Looks like more good news," she announced.

"Should we go back to the lodge for help?" Tina asked her.

"Nah. There was no one at the lodge, remember? That's why we're out here looking for Max. No, you two go on and catch up with the others.

I'll wait here till y'all come back."

"You sure?" I asked.

"It beats hiking," Grandma CeCe said with a grin. Then she slapped herself on the face and said, "Gotcha!"

Just then a staticky voice said, "Okay, Charlie, I think I see the poachers. They're wearing orange vests. There's at least two of them."

We all looked around in amazement. "Where did that come from?" I wondered aloud.

Tina pointed at my walkie-talkie.

"Charlie, this is Dave. Do you read me?" said another staticky voice.

"Maybe they're park rangers," said Tina hopefully.

I yelled into the walkie-talkie, "Help! Please help us!"

The walkie-talkie didn't respond. I fiddled with the knobs and dials.

But the voices had gone away for good.

Dear Pen Pal,

Right after we left Grandma CeCe, we got lost. I don't mean a little lost. I mean totally lost.

When we started out this morning, we were following a trail of potato chips that Max had left. Then we were following what seemed like a regular path in the woods.

But after we left Grandma CeCe it seemed like we were just in the woods. No trail. No nothing.

I checked the map of the place that I had gotten in the lodge. The trail note said to look for piles of three rocks each, called cairns.

We looked for about an hour. I was getting ready to do something useful, like cry. That was when Tina shouted, "Found one!"

We followed the trail markers for a while. But instead of leading us out of the woods, the rocks led us right to the river.

Which is where I am right now.

Tina's off exploring, which doesn't please me too much. Because it means that right now I'm all alone.

EXCEPT FOR ME.

Except for you! Thank you for reminding me, Ghostwriter!

I'll tell you, though. I hope there isn't anyone *else* around besides us two. Maybe it's in my head, but I keep getting the creepy feeling that . . . I'm being watched.

"Gaby!" Tina yelled.

I nearly fell off my rock. I ran down the shore until I found Tina.

She was standing on shore trying to turn over this abandoned old aluminum canoe. I helped her flip it right side up. It looked a little dented, but it floated.

"Tina," I said, "this is perfect." I showed her the map. "This river leads almost all the way to the lodge. I'm sure Kyle or Mom must be around somewhere. We'll just float this out—"

"We don't have a paddle," Tina pointed out.

"Look at the current," I said. "We can drift."

Dragging the canoe into the water was the hard part. Then we loaded our stuff, climbed in, and, sure enough, we started to float.

"Now, this is the way to travel," I said.

"I finally feel like I'm on vacation," Tina joked.

And we've been floating ever since. Right now, I'm lying on the bottom of the canoe. Tina's resting on the other side.

I've got to say, after all the hiking we've been doing, this feels fantastic.

There's just one thing. I feel like we're picking up speed.

I stuffed my diary into my back pocket. Then I sat up. So did Tina. We were really zooming along now. "Look at us go," I said uneasily.

"What's that?" Tina asked.

"What?"

"See? Up there? It looks like the water just stops."

I shielded my eyes against the sun. "Stops? What do you mean?"

"There!" Tina pointed again.

I finally saw what she meant. It was as if someone had cut a line in the water with a razor.

My blood turned cold.

What if the river flowed the other way, not back to the lodge at all?

That would mean we were heading for the waterfall!

"Out!" I screamed. I stood up shakily, trying to hold on to the sides of the canoe. Tina was screaming back, but I couldn't understand what she was saying. "Jump!" I yelled.

I went over one side. Tina went over the other.

The water was freezing. I was swallowing a lot of it. Flailing around. Banging into rocks. My head bobbed up a few times. But not as often as I would have liked!

I couldn't see Tina. But I could see the canoe up ahead. Then it disappeared from sight. Just like that. It must have gone over the falls.

And I was headed the same way.

Up ahead, a dark tree branch was bent over the water, as if reaching out to me. I reached out to grab on to it. Instead the water threw me into the branch with a loud smack.

The branch held. So did I. "Tina!" I screamed. I turned and tried to look behind me. Tina was nowhere to be seen.

Suddenly a hand burst out above the surface of the water. Then a head. Tina was being tossed about as roughly as I had been.

"Tina!" I screamed again as she rushed toward me.

She reached out her hand. I reached out mine. Our hands touched and gripped. I held on with all my might.

By pulling ourselves along that branch, we were able to pull ourselves out of the rapids and out of the river. We lay on the riverbank, drenched and gasping and coughing.

We're still there now, but we're both feeling a lot better. The sun has been drying us off.

We lost all of our stuff, though. The canoe, our walkie-talkies, our backpacks, my watch—everything except my diary and Tina's flashlight. I even lost my Ghostwriter pen. I had to borrow Tina's to write this.

Looks like we're at the base of Hunt's Hill. That's our next plan. When we've got our energy back, we're going to climb it. Maybe from up there we can see where Max is, and the rest of the group.

Maybe.

On the other hand, Tina has been pointing out

to me all the ways that the curse of Hunt's Hill has been coming true. First Max disappears. Then we split off from Alex and Jamal and Lenni. Then Grandma CeCe's ankle. Then the river.

As far as I'm concerned, that's plenty of proof.

What scares me is that we're going to get more proof soon.

Dear Pen Pal,

I thought I was tired before. I didn't know the meaning of the word.

Tina and I have finally made it to the top of Hunt's Hill. We've been lying here like two slabs of meat.

There's no one else up here that we can see. The view is beautiful, just like Max said it would be. But neither of us is really in the mood to enjoy the scenery.

We did find one thing. A campfire that looks as if it was used recently. And a blanket. We hollered but got no answer.

Can things get any worse?

Dear Pen Pal,

I shouldn't have asked that question. The answer is yes. Wait till you hear where I am now.

We were hollering and shouting and yelling. Then we thought we heard something.

"Was that an echo?" Tina said. "Or did somebody answer us?"

We hollered some more, then stopped to listen. At first there was no sound. Then there was a kind of mournful howl. "Some *body* didn't answer us," I said. "Some *thing* did."

"Do raccoons howl?" Tina asked timidly.

As if in response, there was another howl. And another.

"Maybe rabid ones do," I said, "because they're so sick and upset."

Whatever was howling, it sounded like it was getting closer every second.

Then we heard barking.

"Now, I *know* raccoons can't bark," I said.

Then we started running.

When we glanced back over our shoulders, we saw one of the most horrifying sights I've ever seen.

A big black beast of a dog was chasing us with its sharp teeth bared. It was gaining on us fast.

Tina stopped running and shouted, "Up!"

At first I didn't know what she was talking about. What was she suggesting? That we fly?

Tina had knit her fingers together. She held them out for me. "Up!"

The dog was getting closer every second.

Then it dawned on me what Tina wanted. I placed my foot in the support she had made. Tina hoisted me up with all her might. I jumped and caught the lowest tree branch.

The dog was about twenty yards away now and closing fast.

I positioned myself on the branch, then reached down. Tina jumped up and for the second time today she grabbed my hand for dear life. I pulled. She started struggling up the tree trunk.

Then I screamed. The dog was on her. It jumped up and snapped its powerful-looking jaws.

I yanked and Tina surged upward. Still the dog managed to sink its teeth into the seat of her jeans. Lucky for us she was wearing baggy pants!

The dog jumped again. But this time Tina was just out of reach.

We kept climbing. Until the branches got too thin.

And guess what? That dog is still down there. Snarling, drooling, barking, and jumping.

"I love you, tree," Tina says from time to time, patting the trunk.

But how long can we stay here? It's starting to get dark!

GABY—I CHECKED THE ARCHIVES OF THE TOWN LIBRARY. I WAS ABLE TO

CONFIRM MUCH OF THE ED HUNT LEG-
END. HERE IS A LETTER HE WROTE. IT'S
RATHER UNPLEASANT!

To the Town Council:

In response to your rude inquiries, I have
produced the deed to my property. As you
have seen, I own everything from the peak to
the river. I have posted signs all over the land.
Still, hunters and campers continue to
trespass.

If you cannot control your citizens, I will
have to take matters into my own hands. This
is your last warning.

Yours,
Ed A. Hunt

Ghostwriter, thanks. But right now Tina and I
have bigger problems than the legend of Hunt's
Hill. Could you do anything to help us with that
howling beast down there?

I HAVE READ THE DOG'S TAG. HIS
NAME IS BUCK.

Terrific. We're being chased by a ghost dog.
With *real* teeth. Just think: If we waited in this
tree for the rest of our lives, that dog would never
die.

Dear Pen Pal,

Even ghost dogs get bored. It took a long time, but finally Buck gave up and went away.

How far away? That's the question.

I want to stay up here. But Tina is absolutely refusing. I can understand where she's coming from. It's getting darker every second. And she's desperate to find the others.

I have to admit, I'm getting a little anxious myself.

Okay, Buck, here we come. I hope you just gorged yourself somewhere else.

Dear Pen Pal,

It's so dark out I'm writing by flashlight. Tina wants me to turn the light off so that no one will see us. But I'm too scared. And I want to update Ghostwriter.

First things first. We got down from the tree okay. We started making our way back down the peak. Then Tina thought she heard something. We were waiting under a tree, ready to climb it if we had to. I've never listened so hard in my life.

Nothing.

"False alarm," Tina whispered.

"Let's hope so," I said.

"C'mon," she said, touching my arm. "We've got to keep going."

"Maybe we should climb this tree and wait until it gets light out again," I suggested.

"You want to sleep in a tree?"

"Why not?" I said. "Baboons do it. In fact, many animals sleep in trees to protect themselves from predators."

"Fine, Ms. Encyclopedia," Tina said. "But I'm not staying here. You can if you want to."

"That's okay," I said. "I don't feel sleepy."

We started moving forward. We only took one step, though. Because down the hill from us, staring at us with terrifying dark eyes, was a tall figure.

His face was glowing in the darkness, as if the moonlight were making its way through the dark forest just to shine on him. He had a dark mustache. Burning eyes. I didn't have to be told who it was. It was the ghost of Ed Hunt.

I'm proud to say that neither Tina nor I screamed or made any sound.

On the other hand, my heart didn't beat, either. And it's hard to make a sound when you can't even breathe.

Ed Hunt was staring at us with those eyes, just like the eyes Rob described, magnetic eyes that could kill you by looks alone.

Then he slowly raised one hand. He pointed directly at us. "Go!" he commanded in a hollow, ghostly voice.

We didn't need to be told again. We were scrambling through the woods as fast as we could.

We didn't look back. Not even a peek.

We ran until we were completely out of breath. Then we climbed back up into a tree.

Now what?

You know what? I hate to say this, but sometimes I can be one stupid girl. Why didn't I think of this before?

Ghostwriter! This is an emergency! We need to contact Alex, Jamal, and Lenni. At once!

RALLY—G!!!!!!!!

There's just one thing. What if they don't answer?

Reader—Stop! 💣
Do not turn this page!
Gaby's diary ends here.
Do *not* read on until you have turned the book over and read Alex's diary. Then come back to this page and read on to the end.
Otherwise, you will not be able to solve the mystery.
—Ghostwriter

"Alex, turn your flashlight off!" Jamal hissed in the darkness.

"My flashlight isn't on," Alex whispered back.

"Alex," Lenni chimed in. "Stop signaling! The only thing you're going to signal is that crazy beast!"

As if in reply, there was another howl from the darkness. Lenni grabbed Jamal's arm. The three kids were huddled together under a tree just above Hunt's Cave. And from the sound of it, Buck the wild ghost dog was on his way.

Alex shook his head in frustration. Which meant that he happened to glance behind him. It was his diary that was flashing. "Ghostwriter!" Alex exclaimed aloud.

He opened the diary—and gave a tremendous sigh of relief.

Meanwhile, on the other side of Hunt's Hill, two girls were sitting high up in a dark tree.

Gaby was holding the diary. Tina held her flashlight so the light shone tightly on the page.

Finally, the letters moved. "Here we go," said Gaby hopefully. First a *g* flew down toward the white space at the bottom of the page. Then an *a*. Then a group of letters spun in a tight circle and flung themselves out across the page.

GABY? the message finally read. IS THAT REALLY YOU?—ALEX.

Gaby's pen flew.

IT'S ME! AND TINA! ARE YOU OKAY?

The letters glowed as Ghostwriter carried the message to Alex. A second later, the page sparkled as the answer appeared.

YES. OKAY. WE'RE OUTSIDE HUNT'S CAVE. WHERE ARE YOU?

UP A TREE, Gaby wrote back. SOMEWHERE ON HUNT'S HILL.

WHERE ARE ROB AND GRANDMA CECE?

GRANDMA CECE TWISTED HER ANKLE, wrote Gaby. ROB WENT OFF ON HIS OWN. WHERE'S MAX?

The page remained blank for a moment. The answer wasn't much more helpful than the blankness had been. DON'T KNOW.

Gaby and Tina looked at each other. Max had been missing all day.

Their joy at contacting Alex was beginning to fade. What about Rob? Was _he_ okay? Why wasn't he answering Ghostwriter's Rally message?

And what about Grandma CeCe? How could she have made it out of the woods? Was she still sitting out there in the dark?

A message now magically wrote itself into both journals.

I HAVE A MODEST SUGGESTION.

GO AHEAD, Gaby quickly wrote. WHAT? wrote Alex.

I COULD SWAP YOUR DIARIES. THAT WAY, YOU COULD SHARE ALL YOUR INFORMATION. IT MIGHT GIVE YOU SOME CLUES.

This time, neither Gaby nor Alex answered so quickly.

MINE'S VERY PRIVATE, Alex finally answered.

NO WAY, Gaby concluded. TOP SECRET.

The letters spun. THIS IS AN EMERGENCY. UNLESS WE POOL OUR RESOURCES . . .

Ghostwriter let the thought hang unfinished on the page.

"We've got no choice," Tina told Gaby firmly.

"C'mon," Jamal was telling Alex. "What could be so private?"

But it was the next howl from Buck that made Alex decide.

OKAY wrote both brother and sister in their respective diaries.

A moment later, the diary in Gaby's hands began to glow. A fuzzy black ball hovered over the book. Then it was gone.

Gaby gingerly opened the book's cover. There was her diary, just as before. But when she flipped to the first empty page, it was now filled. The page read, *"El Diario Privado de Alejandro Fernandez* (Translation: The Private Diary of Alex Fernandez)."

Gaby gave out an amazed sigh. Then she and Tina moved closer together—and started to read.

"Accept that she's always right," muttered Alex, as he read his sister's diary. "Right!"

"Never mind that stuff," Jamal said over his shoulder. "We don't have time for the two of you to argue now."

About half a mile away, Tina was telling Gaby the exact same thing.

"But look what he says here," Gaby said, miffed. "Me coming along is the one bad thing about the trip!"

"Shush!" Tina commanded. "I'm reading!"

At the same moment, Jamal was tapping Gaby's diary with his forefinger. "Look at this!" He pointed to Gaby's description of the car trip.

"What about it?" Lenni asked.

"I think we followed the wrong trail this morning," he said.

"I could have told you that one, genius," Alex said. "You may have noticed we've been lost all day."

"Jamal," said Lenni. "I don't get it. What about

Gaby's description of the car trip would tell you anything about our trail?"

Attention, Reader! 🎵
Check out Alex's Diary on page 20 and Gaby's Diary on page 6. Can you figure out why Jamal thinks they followed the wrong trail?
—Ghostwriter

Jamal tapped his finger on the page again. "Right here."

Alex and Lenni peered closer. "Max was happily munching on Jamal's plain potato chips," they read. They looked at each other blankly. "So?" Lenni asked Jamal.

"So this morning I thought I had found Max's trail, but I was following a trail of potato chips with lots of green flecks in them. Not plain at all."

"Maybe the chips went bad while they were lying there," Alex suggested. "I don't really see what—"

"Green flecks?" Lenni interrupted. She flipped to another page. "That sounds like sour cream and onion, which Kyle was eating on the dock with Gaby."

Jamal nodded. "I think we followed Kyle, not Max."

"Or maybe," Lenni said, "Kyle tried to throw us off on purpose."

"Why would he do that?" Alex said.

Lenni was writing down their thoughts. Ghostwriter relayed them.

KYLE? WHY WOULD HE DO THAT? Gaby wrote back.

"Well, at least you two agree on something," Lenni teased.

The letters danced on the page as Ghostwriter wrote out another message from Tina and Gaby. THE LODGE HAD ARROWS WITH RED FEATHERS. SAME AS POACHERS?

Alex remembered the arrow whistling past his ear. They turned to the description of the arrows in Gaby's journal. "Looks like more evidence against Kyle," mused Jamal.

"Or just a coincidence," Alex said.

Just then, in the distance, the dog howled again. It was an angry howl.

"Hurry!" Lenni urged.

Tina and Gaby heard the dog's wail as well. "Pick up the pace!" Tina said. But Gaby was lost in thought. "What is it?" Tina demanded.

"So *that's* why he got mad at me," Gaby murmured with a small smile. "He thought I said I would watch the road."

"Will you stop with the argument?" Tina said. She pulled the diary closer to her. Somewhere in the darkness, the dog howled again.

COULD THAT DOG REALLY BE A GHOST? Gaby wrote in the diary.

SOUNDS PRETTY REAL TO ME, Alex wrote back. Gaby couldn't help chuckling.

"Hey!" Gaby said. Tina had grabbed the diary.

"Just a second," Tina said. "I think I remember—"

She looked up. "Just as I thought. That dog isn't Buck after all!"

Attention, Reader!
How did Tina know?
Hint: Study Alex's descriptions of their investigation of Hunt's cabin on page 24 of Alex's Diary. Then look at

Gaby's description of Buck chasing them across Hunt's Hill. See page 36.
—Ghostwriter

"The pen, please," Tina said, holding her hand out.

"Tell me first," Gaby said. But she handed the pen over. It *was* Tina's, after all. Tina wrote down her discovery for Ghostwriter to relay. THE CAPTION AT HUNT'S CABIN SAID BUCK WAS A GOLDEN RETRIEVER. THE DOG THAT'S CHASING US HAS BLACK FUR.

BUT THE NAME TAG SAYS BUCK, Alex wrote back.

"Another coincidence?" Gaby wondered aloud.

"I doubt it," Tina said. "Somebody wants us to think that that legend is true, that these woods are haunted."

"They've got *me* convinced," Gaby lamented.

"But who would want to do this?" Tina said. She wrote down the word SUSPECTS, drew a line under it, then paused. Underneath she wrote down KYLE?

"No way," Gaby said. "Like Alex says, he has no motive."

"You're right," agreed Tina. "It's got to be someone who stands to gain from this place having no campers."

Gaby snapped her fingers. "That letter that I copied into my journal. It was from a possible buyer."

"A buyer would want the price to go as low as possible," said Tina eagerly. She wrote their thoughts down for Ghostwriter.

He quickly transferred them to the other journal.

"Turn back to the letter," Alex told Lenni, who had taken the diary. The three kids studied the letter closely.

"No clues here," Lenni said.

"Except that name," Jamal said. "George Garth. That rings a bell."

Lenni shook her head. "Not for me."

Alex slapped his forehead. "I've got it!"

Attention, Reader! ●
Does the name Garth ring a bell for you as well? Where have you seen it before? (Look at page 13 of Alex's Diary.)
—Ghostwriter

"I wouldn't have remembered if I hadn't kept a diary," Alex said. "But look here—" He riffled the pages, found the spot, and pointed to it.

"The high scorers on that video game at the Lodge. Number one is K. Garth."

"That's not George," Jamal said, bewildered.

"K," said Lenni. "As in Kyle?"

They wrote down their idea for Gaby and Tina, who wrote back, MAYBE KYLE IS GEORGE'S SON.

All this discussion of names jogged something else in Jamal's memory. "Those park rangers Gaby and Tina heard on their walkie-talkies," he said. "What were their names?"

Alex checked. "Charlie and Dave."

Jamal nodded. "And the ranger we talked to was—

"Steve Morrow," remembered Lenni. "Could there be three rangers in such a small area?"

When they wrote this latest finding down for Tina and Gaby, Tina wrote back, YOUR DE-SCRIPTION OF STEVE MORROW MATCHES THE GHOST OF ED HUNT THAT WE SAW.

COME TO THINK OF IT, HE ALSO LOOKED A LITTLE LIKE KYLE, Gaby added.

"So maybe we are looking at father and son,"

Alex told Jamal and Lenni after Ghostwriter relayed the messages.

"And the ranger *we* met could really have been Mr. Garth in disguise," guessed Lenni.

"That would sure explain why he gave us such bad directions," Jamal said. "Those little rock piles were no help. They led nowhere."

"Maybe he and Kyle moved those rock piles to throw us off, to lead us wherever they wanted us to go," Lenni guessed.

Alex grabbed the pen and wrote, GABY AND TINA, STAY PUT. WE'LL COME AND GET YOU.

But Gaby and Tina didn't get the message. Having passed the cave on their way up Hunt's Hill, they were pretty confident they could find it again. They were on their way.

NO RESPONSE, Ghostwriter wrote in Alex's diary.

Alex slammed the diary against a rock. "Why did they stop answering?"

He was getting ready to slam the diary again when Lenni grabbed his arm. She pointed.

Alex couldn't help it. When he saw Gaby's familiar figure emerging from the darkness, his feet started running forward by themselves. He gave her a hug that lifted her right off the ground. Tina was clapping them both on the back.

"By the way," Gaby told Alex with a little smile. "I forgive you for everything bad you wrote about me."

"What about *your* diary?" Alex said with a laugh. "I didn't come off too well in that."

"Okay. I forgive *me* too," Gaby added.

Jamal and Lenni hurried over and the whole group huddled closely together. Still, the night breeze was enough to chill one's bones. Tina shivered. "We've still got to find Rob," she reminded them.

"And my dad," Lenni said grimly.

"And my grandma," Jamal added.

Then Alex spoke the question that had formed in everyone's mind. "How?"

"Here," said Gaby, pulling out her diary. WE COULD USE ANOTHER ONE OF YOUR GREAT SUGGESTIONS, GHOSTWRITER, she wrote. WHICH WAY DO WE GO FROM HERE?

In response, Ghostwriter picked out five letters and dropped them down in one line.

WH CH W O WE GO F OM HERE

I AY D R ?

Then the letters jumped into new positions: DIARY?

"But we've already gone over the diaries," Tina said.

"Then we go over them again," said Jamal.

Taking turns holding the flashlights, the group pored over the two books once again.

It was Alex and Gaby, who were now sharing a diary, who found it first. "The cave!" they both shouted.

Attention, Reader!
Check the descriptions of the cave in the two diaries. Can you spot the fact that doesn't match?
—Ghostwriter

"We thought the cave had two chambers—" explained Alex.

"But the caption on the picture postcard—" continued Gaby.

"Says *three*-chambered," Alex finished. Brother and sister grinned at each other.

"Let's go!" Jamal said. Even as he said it, he was already heading back toward the cave.

The bats were fluttering around like crazy this time. But the group kept going, all the way to the back of the second chamber.

"So where's this third chamber?" Tina said. She sat down on a boulder.

"Must have been a misprint," Jamal said.

"Dad!" Lenni screamed.

They listened. And heard a muffled pounding. It was coming from behind the boulder Tina was sitting on.

Tina jumped off the rock and the kids all gathered around. They put their shoulders to one side of the stone. "One, two, three," counted Jamal. "Push!"

At first the rock didn't budge. "Push!" Jamal kept shouting.

Grunting, they finally managed to get the rock rolling.

Behind it lay a narrow, dark tunnel. Lenni fell to her knees and started crawling forward. Jamal followed.

Alex was about to follow him when he heard distant shouting. It sounded happy. A few minutes later, Jamal crawled back out.

Followed by Lenni.

Followed by . . .

Max.

"Thank God!" Max was saying as he hugged the kids. "It was the craziest thing. I was spelunking in the third chamber and then I couldn't find my way out."

"Spelunking?" Alex asked.

"Cave exploring," Gaby said proudly.

Alex shook his head. "She knows everything."

Lenni kept hugging her dad. "The Garths probably rolled this boulder in behind you to give you a scare," she told him.

"The Garths?" asked Max. "Who are the Garths?"

Before anyone could explain, Jamal hissed a loud warning. "Shhhh!"

The reason for the warning was soon clear. There were other voices in the cave. And they were coming right toward Max and the team.

"Get back in the tunnel!" ordered Alex.

But before anyone had time to move, two powerful flashlight beams like headlights trapped the group.

"Mr. Frazier?" called a voice.

"It's Mom!" yelled Gaby.

"Mom?" Alex said, peering into the darkness.

"Not *our* mom!" laughed Gaby.

Mom Brody now emerged from the blinding light of the flashlights. Next to her were the two real park rangers that Gaby had overheard on the walkie-talkie—Charlie and Dave.

"Boy, am I glad to see you all in one piece," Mom boomed.

"Where is my grandmother?" Jamal demanded.

"Your grandmother is back at the Lodge," Dave told Jamal. "Her ankle's a little tender, and her poison ivy is fierce—"

"But other than that, she's fine," said the ranger named Charlie.

"We're still missing Rob," Lenni said.

"Rob?" asked Dave.

"Another kid in our group," explained Max.

Tina had taken one of the diaries. She was scribbling a frantic note to Rob. Ghostwriter relayed it, but as usual there was no answer. She looked at the other kids and shook her head.

"We've been through the whole area today—" began Charlie.

"We covered Mom's whole map," agreed Dave. "We didn't see him."

The whole map? Gaby grabbed a flashlight from Jamal and studied her diary. A moment later, she exclaimed, "Got it!"

She was holding one of the diaries open to show the two maps—the one she got in the Lodge and the one Alex got from Max. "I think I know where we should look," she said.

Attention, Reader! 💣

Study the two maps closely (page 2 of Alex's Diary and page 16 of Gaby's Diary). What place was left off Gaby's map?

—Ghostwriter

The whole group gathered around Gaby. "See? The new maps don't show this tree house," she explained.

"Gaby, that doesn't mean anything," said Alex. "It could have been torn down."

"Maybe," said Gaby. "But I bet the Garths changed the map to hide it."

"The Garths?" asked Mom, shocked.

"We'll explain on the way," Jamal said urgently. "Please—let's go!"

"Sounds worth a look," said Dave.

"This way," Charlie said, shining his flashlight as he led them back out of the cave.

Several hundred yards from the mouth of the cave sat two big Land Rovers. "Pile in," Dave said.

"You mean we went through the woods and there were roads?" Lenni said, amazed.

"Not roads, exactly. But there are some trails that'll get us partway there," said Dave.

The rangers drove fast through the dark forest. Then they parked and the group set out on foot again. It was a twenty-minute trek through the dense, dark brush before they reached the tree house.

Which was right where the old map said it would be.

When Alex saw the wooden rungs hammered into the tall trunk, he broke into a run. He was the first one up the ladder.

It was a long climb. Above him was a vast cabin that was fully hidden within a mass of dark leaves.

Inside the cabin, the first thing Alex noticed was a ranger uniform on a wire hanger.

Then he turned and saw Rob, bound and gagged in a chair.

Alex ran to him and worked at the gag as the rangers and the rest of the team came up into the room.

"Oh, wow," Rob said as soon as the gag came off. "Am I glad you're here! First these guys tried to convince me they were ghosts! But when that didn't work they tied me up. They're—"

A sharp gesture from one of the rangers cut him off in midsentence.

They heard the sound of voices, approaching the bottom of the tree.

The voices came steadily closer.

Everyone stood very still, waiting. Soon, the voices became understandable. "Kyle, my boy," said the older voice. "I think our work is almost done. I predict Mom will sell this place to me by the end of the week. For nothing."

"Far out!"

"Then we can cut down the whole woods, sell the lumber, and make a bundle."

"Dad," said the other voice. "Quiet. The kid."

"Oh, right."

The voices grew silent. For several moments, the only sounds were the sounds of feet scraping against the wooden rungs of the tree house ladder. Then the dark-haired head of George Garth, alias the ghost of Ed A. Hunt, came into view. When he had climbed all the way into the cabin, he noticed the ring of faces. He froze.

64

"The ghosts are back, kid," Kyle was saying, as he climbed up after his father.

"Actually, the ghosts are under arrest," Charlie told him.

Dear Pen Pal,

We're on our way back to New York, riding in our old friend the blue whale of a van. I got the front window seat again, but in return I have to study the map and navigate.

I can't believe how well everything worked out.

The Garths confessed to everything, from moving the cairns to sending us those phony smoke messages. And the rangers said they're going to make Mr. Garth pay Mom for all her lost business. Excellent!

Even more amazing: I'm getting along with Alex.

—Except that Gaby says we should go left at the next turnoff, when I know we should go right.

Ha! Alex wrote that last line. Someday he will learn that I am always right. After all, wasn't I right on the ride up? Left definitely takes us back to New York. I just told Max for the sixth time.

Good, he turned left.

But . . . I just had a bad thought.

Maybe left leads to Smoky Swamp?